C000050509

MELODY JAMES
a novella

MELODY JAMES
Stephen Gallagher

THE BROOLIGAN PRESS
LONDON
NEW YORK

First Publication

This edition published 2018 by The Brooligan Press
Rights and Permissions: Howard Morhaim Literary Agency
30 Pierrepont St, Brooklyn NY 11201

ISBN: 978 1 9999207 8 4

For Bill Schafer, who gave me the push, and Shaye Areheart,
who opened the way

ONE

"WE HAVE a man. We want to know if we can trust him and I think you can get us the answer."

These words were addressed to a woman of deceptive youth by Sir Anthony Gair Rathbone, the British government's Assistant Director of Intelligence, one long-ago afternoon in the drawing room of Blackpool's grand Hotel Metropole. It was the bitter winter of 1919, one full year after the ending of the Great War. Rathbone and his civil service companion had travelled up from London with the purpose of securing the young woman's services.

But I get ahead of myself.

My name is Sebastian Becker. In 1926 I would be sent to interview Gair Rathbone—Gerry to his friends and family, Sir Anthony to all others—after the incident in Hyde Park that ended his career. That interview would lead me to uncover this episode in his past.

Which really begins in South Norwood, at the 1919 October fair.

TWO

SIR ANTHONY Gair Rathbone, then a bachelor in his 40s, was calling on his sister's family at their Auckland Road villa. During his visit, his favourite niece developed a sudden eagerness to take a walk out to the fairgrounds. No one in the family shared her enthusiasm, so Rathbone volunteered to accompany her.

On the way, she confided her motive.

"What if she's not here this year, Uncle Gerry?" she said when she'd explained her reasons. "Or it's someone else, not as good?"

"It barely matters, Lucy," Rathbone told her. "It's all the same nonsense."

"You say that. But when Millicent was getting those letters, this is the one who told her the man's name."

"There's no doubt in my mind that Millicent blabbed her suspicions and the psychic simply said yes."

"Well, I won't do anything of the kind."

"Of course not."

This was the last afternoon of the fair, and there was a healthy crowd in attendance. The attractions had been pitched close to railway lines at the recreation ground's southern end. There was an outer ring of portable sideshow buildings, all brightly painted and elaborately decorated, folding cathedrals that could be collapsed onto their wagon bases in less than an hour. Each one had a platform out front and a promise of wonders within, all surrounding a compact village of rides, tents,

Gavioli organs, and a steam carousel. The enclosure was entered through a mighty gateway, actually a painted façade made of sticks and canvas.

Lucy held onto her uncle's arm as they made their way through the press of South London people, craning to scan every banner and painted sign as she went.

She said, "I don't see her, Uncle Gerry. Will you ask someone for me?"

So Rathbone caught the attention of a money-taker on the Swinging Boats, who cocked an ear to his question then called out "Jack!" A dozen heads turned, and his call brought another man over. Where the money-taker worked in shirtsleeves and a waistcoat, this man wore a brown suit with a collar and tie. But his shoes were unpolished and there was grime under his fingernails. He might have been handsome when young, but with approaching middle age came a beefy frame and a drinker's complexion.

The money-taker returned to his Swing Boats and Rathbone said, "We're looking for the fortune teller."

"Are you now," this man Jack said, and waited for more.

"The one named Melody?" Lucy ventured. "It's for a private reading."

Jack looked from one to the other. He said, "Miss James doesn't take money for readings."

"But she'll sell us a book for a guinea," Lucy said. "I understand how it works."

Jack glanced at Rathbone, weighing both of them up, and then nodded for them to follow. He led without looking back and they had to make their own way through the crowd, dodging shopgirls and clerks and jostled by an overexcited simpleton of indeterminate age chasing a paper fancy.

They reached a relatively quiet area of caravans and tents by plane trees away from the rides. The ground was soft here, unsuitable for the big wagons, and rush mats had been laid down to create pathways where the mud was at its worst. Jack stopped by a plain canvas tent that carried no signage or banner. He raised the flap and said, "Wait in here."

They stepped inside. The man did not follow, but let the flap fall.

The tent was on the small side; a dozen people at most might have crowded into it. A table and four chairs stood on bare grass at its centre and on the table stood an oil lamp, unlit. Beside the lamp were a tattered deck of ordinary playing cards and a small stack of cheaply printed pamphlets.

Rathbone picked up one of the pamphlets as Lucy drew out a chair but didn't sit. The paper was coarse, the ink smudged. It was a treatise on palm reading.

"A guinea," he mused, and tossed the pamphlet back onto the table.

"It's worth it to me," Lucy said.

"I can tell you what you need to hear for nothing," Rathbone said. "Marry the banker. Choose the artist and you'll end up feeding all his friends with your father's money."

"Very level-headed of you, Uncle Gerry," Lucy said, "but I don't expect you to understand."

Both then turned at the sound of canvas being raised.

A woman stood in an opening at the back of the tent, holding the flap; one of the travelling folk, she wore a thick cotton blouse and a heavy wool skirt with buttons, her boots splashed with mud. No rings, no shawl, no headscarf, none of the usual fortune-teller's trappings. And young. She might easily have been taken for a girl of fifteen or sixteen, though her bearing was of one much older.

She said, "Whose is the reading?"

Unable to resist, Rathbone said, "Shouldn't you be telling us?"

Lucy shot her uncle a look and said, "That will be me."

The young woman treated Rathbone to a brief gaze before moving forward into the tent, letting the canvas fall shut behind her.

Turning to Lucy she said, "I don't speak to the dead. If that's what you're looking for, then I can't help you."

"It's not that," Lucy said.

"And you understand the arrangement?"

Lucy had a small purse ready. From it she counted out eight half-crowns and a shilling onto the table, then looked up at the young woman.

"I don't need the book," she said.

"Take the book," Melody James said, "or I can't do the reading. No offence, but I won't break the law."

Rathbone cut in and said, "I'm not here to entrap you, if that's what you're thinking."

"That much I do know," the young woman said, and gestured for them to sit.

Lucy took the chair that she'd pulled out, and Rathbone the one next to it. The teller was right to be wary. Under the Vagrancy Act, soliciting money for palmistry or fortune-telling with intent to deceive could land her three months' hard labour or a twenty-five pound fine.

Melody James went around and took another seat for

herself, to face them across the table.

She reached for the playing cards and slid the pack across to a spot in front of Lucy. She said, "I want you to shuffle the cards and then cut them with your left hand only. Two heaps, and they don't have to be equal."

They waited with patience as Lucy gave the cards an inexpert shuffle. During this brief interlude, Rathbone said to Melody. "You're very young."

"I know I appear so to some," she replied, her eyes on the cards as Lucy managed the awkward left-handed cut.

The teller then took both heaps and removed the top card of each, before recombining the rest and squaring up the deck. From the deck she dealt three piles of ten cards each.

"These cards represent your past," she said, touching the first pile and then moving to the next. "These your present. This your future. Which would you have me read?"

"The future," Lucy said. "I have a specific question."

"Don't tell it to me."

She pushed the unwanted cards aside, then turned the remaining pile over and spread it. After examining the faces of the cards she began to re-sort them to make pairs and triplets.

"Your question is one of romance," she said as she moved them around. "The two of hearts tells me that there are rivals. These paired cards, the King and Jack of Clubs, represent indifference and favour. So you have two suitors. You favour one and you don't care for the other. Yet you're asking for guidance."

Lucy was about to respond, but then she caught a glance from her uncle and remained tight-lipped.

Melody James went on, "The two of diamonds for happiness, the ten of clubs for benefit. But the ten is reversed. Do you see where this is going?"

This time, Lucy couldn't help herself.

"I do," she said.

"Your head tells you one, your heart the other. Your choice is between security and happiness."

"So what should I do?"

"I can't tell you which choice to make, but the cards can point to what the outcome will be. Do you wish to know?"

"I do."

Rathbone hadn't looked at the cards, not even once; he kept all his attention on Melody James, watching her work, studying her method. For her part, she appeared to ignore Rathbone completely. She spoke only to Lucy, with the politician's knack of engaging a stranger so that the listener felt like the most important person in the world. Lucy, he could see, was completely taken in.

The teller looked down at the two cards set aside from that first, left-handed cut.

She said, "Choose one to be your fortune card, and turn it."

Lucy took a long time to decide, as if momentous issues really were in play. As if this choice might even determine the course of a life. Rathbone felt his heart move with an absurd cocktail of pity and love.

"Just choose," Melody said.

Lucy turned one of the cards. It was the King of Hearts.

She said, "Does that mean what I think it means?"

"They never mean what you think they mean," Melody said. "The King of Hearts is the card of hurt."

"Oh," Lucy said. "So what's my answer?"

"Be willing to have regrets."

Something happened in the next few moments, and Rathbone couldn't be sure what it was. He saw their eyes meet, and an understanding pass between the two. It was an exchange in the private language of young women, an understanding that seemed unforced and genuine, and from which he was excluded.

The King of Hearts lay on the table before them.

"I think I see where this leads me," Lucy said.

Rathbone said drily, "I'm sure her father will thank you for this."

"He can thank the cards," Melody said. "I only say what they show. Would you like a reading for yourself?"

"For another guinea?"

"I can let you decide what it's worth."

His answer was no, but somehow his ready refusal didn't surface as quickly as it might. She slid the reassembled pack in front of him and by then it was too late. He had reached the point where to back out might look like mere cowardice.

Her gaze was on him. It was steady. He met it for a while, then reached to shuffle and cut the pack. He believed he understood her method. It was a confidence game with a very old art to it, the art of dressing common wisdom to make it seem specific to the subject. Lucy had taken the reading one way. Another might hear the same words and find their own, equally accurate meaning in them.

As before, Melody set aside two cards, dealt three piles, and this time took the centre hand.

"You're not telling my future?" Rathbone said.

"Where would be the point in that?" she said. "I

could tell you anything, and be long gone before you could fault me. Is this not supposed to be a test?"

She turned the cards face-up and spread them, sorting pairs and triples as before. Apparently these had some significance. She took her time. Such was the nature of this theatre, he thought. Rathbone glanced at Lucy, who was following every one of the teller's moves with intense interest.

Melody James looked up at him.

"Well?" he said.

"A lost love," she said. "A sad loss, a long time ago. There's never been another."

"Stay out of the past," he said. "Stick to the present."

"It's a loss that shapes your present because you can't forget. Your niece is not unlike her. Perhaps the reason why you play the doting uncle?"

"No."

"She means Luciana, Uncle Gerry," his niece put in, all promises of discretion forgotten in her excitement. Then, to Melody James; "I'm named for her."

"Move on."

That did not come out as he'd intended. He had not meant to snap.

Melody returned her attention to the cards. She frowned and said, "There are two lives presented here. I'm not sure I understand."

"I'm sure you don't."

Melody seemed to sense his discomfort and looked at him directly.

She said, "Do the people around you know the truth of what you do?"

"Meaning?"

Melody glanced at Lucy, making a point that would

not be lost on Rathbone. She said, "I won't pretend to understand your trade. But I see duplicity in it."

"Duplicity?"

"But in some official capacity. Do you want me to say more?"

"No," Rathbone said. "I think we're done."

"Then turn the last card," Melody said. "It may resolve the question without you having to speak."

Despite himself, Rathbone moved as if to reach for one of the two cards lying separate from the rest. But then he stopped and, instead, pushed back his chair and rose to his feet.

"No," he said, "the amusements are over. Good day to you, Miss . . . James? You have a very clever act."

"Uncle Gerry!" Lucy said, in a rare tone of reproof.

"It's a statement of fact," Rathbone said. "Take it any other way and I can only apologise. Come on, Lucy."

He dug around in his pocket, and produced a shilling which he threw onto the table.

"For the entertainment," he said, and then ushered a bewildered Lucy out of the tent, leaving their fortune teller alone with her payment and her playing cards.

THREE

MELODY JAMES gathered all but one of her pasteboards and squared the deck one last time, straightening the odd bent corner and crease. It was an old deck of her uncle Jack's, useless for gambling because at least one third of the cards could be identified from their backs by marks or damage. But fine for the cartomancy, where age and wear gave them a sense of mystical authority. And while Melody James had no belief in luck or supernatural influence, familiar objects gave her a sense of reassurance. It was all a part of life on the road in an ever-changing world.

She waited a few moments until she could no longer hear the voices of her clients outside, and was about to call to Jack when he popped through the canvas at the back of the tent.

"A shilling?" he said indignantly. "The tight b—"

"Where's Alfie?" Melody said.

Alfie Hewitt, last seen in the role of a simpleton pursuing a paper fancy, ducked in after Jack. He was an undersized boy of around fifteen, sharp as a tack, quick as a whippet, grubby as a printer's thumb. From her skirts under the table Melody produced a gentleman's expensive wallet and card case, in monogrammed leather with silver corners. She held it out.

"Get this back into his coat before he looks for it," she said, adding, "Something of hers would have been a lot more use."

"I tried for her purse," Alfie protested, "but she put a

right grip on it."

"Go."

Jack took swipe at Alfie's head as he ran out, and Melody said, "Leave him."

"What if His Nibs had reached for his wallet to pay for the reading?"

"What if, what if," Melody said.

Alfie could be trusted to return Rathbone's property without raising suspicion. Either with a second brush-by, or through some other spur-of-the-moment devious means. Though born of showman's stock, Alfie was an orphan who lived on his considerable wits. He'd joined the James family for the South East leg of their season, working for meals and board and whatever small change he could make on the side.

Melody waved Jack out, and then contemplated the one remaining playing card that lay apart from the pack and face-down on the table. In the absence of any useful intelligence on the lovely Lucy, Melody had waited and listened through the canvas for a few moments to get a steer on the girl's thinking. She hadn't needed long. A pretty young woman's struggle over a choice between suitors was older than Shakespeare, and there was a ready routine for it.

She probably shouldn't have given in to the temptation to offer a further reading, but Sir Anthony Gair Rathbone's aggressive scepticism had made it hard for her to resist. Especially given the information that Alfie's light fingers had placed into her hands just ahead of their arrival. A quick dip into the wallet had revealed, besides the usual banknotes, a small glassine envelope protecting a lock of hair and a hand-coloured picture, Victorian in style. The picture showed a young woman, fair of skin, in a pale blue dress and bearing more than a passing resemblance to Lucy.

A teller could never go wrong with love and loss, but it was Rathbone's government credentials that had inspired her more daring proposition. By his reaction, she'd landed her shot.

Before her on the table was his last card, the one he'd begun to reach for but wouldn't turn.

Melody turned it now. The Ten of Clubs.

Clubs were never good. In Madame Lenormande's method of divination, the ten was the card of betrayal.

"The treachery card?" Melody said aloud. "Perhaps there's something in this moonshine after all."

TWO MORE dates to play, and then the weather closed in. November saw the James family pack up the swing boats, the two shies, the barrel organ and the ghost show, and retire to their regular winter quarters on the Lancashire coast. Blackpool mostly stood empty in the off-season, and space was cheap. The rides and the caravans went into rented storage on the South Shore, while employees dispersed to their own families and the Jameses moved into the guest house managed by Melody's Aunt Florence.

It was their first ever permanent winter base. Melody had bought the house with the proceeds from the sale of her father's Wild West act, and last year had picked up a second property in Great Yarmouth. She'd been the family's *de facto* business head since the age of seventeen. Though her judgement wasn't perfect—a short-lived broomstick marriage at sixteen was testimony to that—she was the rightful heir and it had quickly become clear that her business sense was sound.

Florence had wanted only to get off the road, and her sister Lottie had a growing family to occupy her. And Lottie's husband Jack . . . well, Jack was Jack, and if he could be relied upon for anything, it was his capacity for letting you down.

The house was a tall mid-terrace in a street of similar guesthouses behind the Winter Gardens. Offering six bedrooms with attic rooms above and a useful cellar below, it was proving a good investment. Every northern town had its Wakes Week, when factories closed and entire families relocated to the coast. Through the summer season they came to Blackpool in their thousands, arriving in waves on Holiday Specials at the town's three railway stations. The Blackpool landladies gave them breakfast and sent them out for the day, forbidden to return before six o'clock. They sat on the beach on their Sunday best, undid a button or two, spent all their savings on low-cost entertainments, then journeyed home to count the weeks until next summer's holiday. Florence took bookings from Easter to October, which left the house empty in the off-season for the James family's use.

It was on a Wednesday morning in late November that Melody, after bringing the books up to date and writing two letters to the bank, made her way down to the scullery at the back of the house where her Aunt Florence was folding laundry from a ceiling rack.

Melody said, "Any news on Jack?"

"Lottie's heard nothing," Florence said.

"Where is she?"

"Out looking for him."

All were concerned about Jack; or rather, Lottie was concerned about Jack, and was determined to co-opt everyone else into her anxiety. Jack had married into the family, was the father of Lottie's children, and no one disputed the fact that his place was among them; but he was a disappointed man, a boozer and a gambler, and this wasn't his first overnight absence.

"I'll ask around," Melody said.

After stopping by the Post Office with her letters she walked along Abingdon Street to the Railway Hotel, where her uncle was well known. There was a brewer's dray at the yard entrance and Frank, the pub's pot-man and general handyman, was helping a drayman to unload barrels with ropes, ramp, and a dirty cushion.

The public house would have been Lottie's first call in the search for her husband, but Melody knew Frank and she knew the rest of the Railway Hotel crowd. If a man's wife made enquiries and infidelity was involved, they'd all feign ignorance. Jack had strayed before. When he went off with other women Lottie would blame them, not him, and always took him back.

Melody said, "Have you had any sight of our Jack? No flannel, now. It's not Lottie you're talking to."

"God's truth no, Melody," Frank said, sweating despite the cold and gasping from the effort of hoisting oak. "But someone's been looking for you."

"Me?"

"Two posh gents from London. They're asking everywhere. Left a card on the bar."

"What's it about?"

Frank waved his hand vaguely, having reached the limit of the breath that he could muster. "Better ask the boss," he said.

She went inside and sought out the landlord, who found the card in question and handed it across the counter. He told her that he'd been waiting to give the message to Jack for delivery—better that, he'd reckoned, than send strangers to her doorstep.

"Engraved," the landlord said as she read the card. "That's a sign of class, that is."

Two posh gents. Melody had been approached by such types before, usually public-school men from well-funded betting syndicates believing that a psychic could give them an easy edge. Though not averse to taking money from fools, she preferred to avoid those fools who might go on to give her serious trouble.

This could be different. She recognised the name *Sir Anthony Gair Rathbone KBE.* Below the name was a four-digit Mayfair telephone number. In the white space below the number was handwritten the name of the resort's Hotel Metropole.

She said, "What did they want?"

"Wouldn't say," the landlord told her. "Other than that there's money in it."

FOUR

THE TRAVELLING life had trained Melody James in suspicion, but if there was money in the offing, she would know more. Jack and his problems could wait.

The Hotel Metropole was a substantial redbrick building between the promenade and the sea, close to the Tower and the Central Pier and so situated that the tramlines swung inland to avoid it. The interior was as grand as its name, and its clientele's interests more inclined to *haute cuisine* and spa treatments than donkey rides and Punch and Judy shows. The Imperial might be bigger, smarter, and the preferred choice of Royalty, but for now it was out of bounds to the gentry; wartime use as an officers' hospital had left it in need of a refit.

Melody presented herself at the Metropole's front desk and showed the visiting card to the clerk.

The clerk looked her over and said, "What's it about?"

And she replied, "How's it your business?"

"You want to see him or not?"

"Fine," she said, "tell him you turned me away," and reached to take it back.

At that, and with bad grace, he called a young page over. "Find Sir Anthony," he said, handing him the card. "I think he's in the billiard room. Show him this and ask if he'd care to come out."

"I'll go in," Melody said.

"No you won't."

Though not invited to sit, she unbuttoned her coat and went over to take a seat on one of the lobby's fancy and French-looking chairs. Within a minute Sir Anthony Gair Rathbone appeared in the lobby, followed by another man pulling on his jacket.

"Miss James," Rathbone said, extending his hand. "Do you remember me?"

"I do," she said, taking it. Though his appearance was the same, his manner was markedly different to that of their other meeting.

He said, "This is my colleague, Mister Grenville."

Grenville nodded, and didn't offer his hand. He had the doleful face and watery eyes of a loose-skinned hound. She disliked him on sight.

Melody said, "I'd care to know why you've been papering the front with my name."

"We have a proposal for you."

"*Your* proposal, Gair," the other man threw in, as if unwilling to have anyone overhear and assume that he shared responsibility.

"As you prefer, Oswald," Rathbone said evenly, and then, to Melody, "Mister Grenville doesn't set much store by psychics and clairvoyants."

"I'm neither," Melody said.

"Of course not. Which is exactly why we're here." He looked to the desk clerk. "We'll take tea in the drawing room," he said.

"I don't have the time," Melody said. "I've got family business. Can't you just state yours?"

"It's a matter of service to your country. Please. We travelled up from London just to find you."

"Money's been mentioned."

Grenville lifted his chin and said, "I thought that

might do it."

Ignoring his colleague, Rathbone gestured as if to guide her toward the lounge.

"Please," he said again. His manner seemed genuinely respectful, but Melody was not taken in. Rathbone was of a class to whom courtesy came easily, regardless of sincerity.

Nevertheless, she went along. They moved through into a drawing room that was decorated in a Moorish style, at odds with its window views of the cold grey ocean. Again Rathbone offered afternoon tea, and again Melody declined. If Rathbone was out to put her at ease, she wanted to know why.

He explained, "We have a man. We want to know if we can trust him and I think you can get us the answer. I'm no more a believer in the occult than Grenville, here, but I can't deny that you have a gift."

"A gift you valued at no more than a shilling."

"I apologise for that. You were more accurate than you can know. I'll confess it disturbed me."

Grenville cut in with an impatient, "Can we get to business?"

"Tell me what you want from me," Melody said, "and I'll tell you what it's worth."

"This man I mentioned to you. He's in a position to perform a service to the nation but we can't be sure where his loyalties lie. We need to know, can we trust him with our interests in a foreign land? He'll be as well-placed to betray us as to serve."

"Are we talking about the Russian situation?"

"What do you know of that?" Grenville said sharply.

"I know a family of aerialists who can't return home because the Bolsheviks killed their grandparents and took the farm. And there's talk of a tumbler with Fosset's who joined the White Guards."

"Then," Rathbone said, "you already know more than we'd intended."

Grenville said, "Time's a'wasting, Gair. We need an answer."

But Melody wasn't ready to offer one. "Where's your spy now?" she said. "Is he with you?"

"You'll have to travel."

"To Russia?"

"To London."

"I can't go to London. I have rides to overhaul and a season to plan."

Grenville said, "Surely that's a man's job."

Having largely ignored him so far, Melody turned to Grenville now. "My father's dead and my husband's gone," she said. "And yet I seem to manage."

"We'll get you there and fetch you back," Rathbone said. "I can't see it taking you away for more than three days or so. Surely you can spare us that."

Melody considered for a moment and then said, "Fifty pounds."

"For telling a fortune?" Grenville said. "I thought the going rate was a guinea."

"We'll pay you twenty," Rathbone said. "And cover your fares and lodging."

"It's fifty," Melody said, rising. "I'll let you think about it."

With a nod to each of them, she turned and headed for the way out. Grenville called after her, "If you loved your country you'd do it for nothing."

"If my country loved me," she fired back across the room, "I'd have the vote."

*   *   *

WHEN MELODY returned to the house she was met by Florence in the hallway, carrying freshly pressed linen for the bedrooms. "Lottie's in the back," Florence said. "She's had news."

"Is Jack all right?"

"She'll tell you."

There was disapproval in her Aunt's tone. Melody went on through, and found Lottie at the kitchen table. She'd been crying. Not through grief or even relief; these were angry tears. Her eldest, six-year-old Lily, stood by her in silence, patting her arm.

"He went pitching pennies in the dunes," Lottie said. "The police picked him up. That's why he didn't come home."

"Pitch and toss? At this time of year?"

"And he'll have lost all his money. Like he always does."

The game was played in the sandy hills out towards St Anne's where the last of the old gypsy camps had stood. A pitch and toss school was a loud, raucous affair, and the dunes made an ideal location. As many as a hundred men could gather to watch and place bets on the fall of three coins. Lookouts would be posted on the tops so the gamblers could scatter at any raid. Most would escape while the unlucky were caught, and Jack was invariably one of the unluckiest.

His most likely punishment would be a ten pound fine. Lottie couldn't afford it, so Melody would no doubt be standing him the cash.

And at least it wasn't a woman this time. Melody held

back from offering this as a comfort. Lottie knew that Jack was useless, but fiercely resented it if anyone else ever said so.

"Well," Melody said, "you'll have him back soon enough. A night in a police station may have calmed him down a bit."

"You don't understand," Lottie said. "Now he's in the hospital!"

"What happened?"

"A fight in the cells. I don't know how bad he is. They won't let me see him."

"Was drink involved?"

"You're all quick to blame him. No one ever takes his side!"

"Where is he? Is he at the Vic?"

Lottie nodded, miserably.

"I'll see what I can find out," Melody said.

FIVE

THE BLACKPOOL Victoria Hospital, known to all as The Vic, had opened on Whitegate Lane in 1894. It was built in a style that mashed together High Gothic and Queen Anne Revival to resemble a haunted mansion outgrowing its grounds.

Melody was wondering what she might find when she located Jack; although she'd avoided being too grave around Lottie, who was upset enough already, the fact that the police had moved him to the Vic was a cause for concern. The local coppers were not soft. The most a man could usually expect after a prison beating would be an unsympathetic once-over from the police doctor and a damp cloth to press on the bruises.

Much as she expected, on first enquiry she was told that a man in police custody was here under guard and no visitors were allowed. And no, they couldn't tell her where in the building he was being held. As soon as his treatment was completed he'd be moved back to police cells in the courthouse.

Melody whispered a meek thanks and took herself away. Once outside she squared her shoulders, went around the side, and re-entered with the kitchen staff.

Jack was at the back end of the men's ward, and not so hard to find because there was a uniformed police-man on a chair beside him.

Melody stopped as if in passing and said to the officer, "Did the Irish nurse find you?"

"The Irish nurse?" the policeman said. "What did

she want?"

"Didn't say, but it was you she wanted."

He rose. One of the older men on the local force, he was six feet tall with a wide belt around his broad middle. His moustache was a full walrus.

He said, "Watch him. Shout if he moves," and went off in search of the mythical Irish nurse, of which the Vic no doubt had several.

Jack was safe to be left without guard for a while. He was in a hospital nightshirt and shackled to the bed.

Even though prepared for the sight of him, Melody was shocked. He'd been so badly beaten that he was barely recognisable, his lips split and both eyes swollen completely shut.

She stood over him and said, "Can you see me, Jack?"

He made the effort and turned his head a little to bring her into view.

"What are you doing here?" he said.

"Who did this to you?"

Jack's answer was a what's-the-point sigh, but Melody persisted. "Who did this, Jack?"

"It was the Brugnetti brothers."

"Why?"

"I don't want to say."

"You're going to tell me, Jack. Or else I'll go to the Brugnettis and get *them* to explain."

One piece at a time, and knowing that time was limited, she got the story out of him.

He'd been one of a number arrested in a sweep operation on the pitch and toss school. He'd been put in a cell with the brothers from one of the town's most notorious families, where the custody sergeant had 'just happened by' and revealed that they'd seized 'sweated' coins in the course of the raid. Sweated coins were like marked cards, doctored and weighted to fall in a predictable way. As soon as the sergeant had gone, the brothers had turned on Jack as he'd known they would.

"But why you?" Melody said.

"Because they were my bad pennies," he admitted. "I organised the school."

"Oh, Jack."

"I've got so many debts! I needed quick money!"

"But you didn't come to me. You reckoned you'd swindle it out of the most dangerous family in town."

"It nearly worked," he said.

"Your schemes always nearly do," she said, "but you never seem to learn."

"It's prison for me this time, Melly."

"What do I tell Lottie?"

"Tell her I'm sorry, and to stay away. I don't want the little ones to see me like this."

It was at this point that the officer returned, slightly perplexed and somewhat suspicious, and to avert those suspicions Melody said, "Did you find her?"

"No. Did he give you any trouble?"

"He's got troubles enough," Melody said, and yielded the chair.

Here was a problem that no amount of cash would solve. One couldn't simply buy off a Brugnetti in a temper. At the age of eleven—or so it was rumoured—one of the boys had kicked a tramp to death under the Victoria Pier, leaving the body to be carried out on the next tide. Grandfather Brugnetti was a glassmaker from the old country. Fancy glass was still the family business, but only for the sake of appearances. The family's money now came from other, less reputable activities.

She could see only one way forward, and it meant a return to the Metropole. But providence saved her from the journey; outside in the corridor, only a few steps away from the ward, she found her way blocked by Sir Anthony Gair Rathbone.

"Miss James," he said. This time, he was alone.

"How did you find me?

"I want to apologise for my colleague. He was less than gracious. He thinks this entire trip's a fool's errand. We'll meet your fee. I'll make up the difference myself."

"There's no need for that," she said. "I'll take your twenty plus a favour."

"Oh?"

"You're a man of influence. I need my uncle kept out of prison."

Rathbone glanced toward the long room she'd just left, and listened as she explained her reasons.

He said, "That's not how the justice system works."

"Come on, Sir Anthony," she said. "We both know how it *really* works. If it was some toff's brother he'd never have seen the inside of a cell."

"He wouldn't be caught gambling for pennies on a beach, either."

"No, he'd be swindling the bookies at Royal Ascot, but it all amounts to the same. His name's Jack. If he ends up in gaol with the Brugnetti brothers, he won't be coming out."

And so the deal was done, there in a corridor of Blackpool's Victoria Hospital. Rathbone gave her money for a train ticket and the address of a hotel in London, with instructions to make her way there the next day and wait to be contacted.

*　　　*　　　*

THERE'S MUCH I could tell you about Melody James, most of it perhaps best saved for another time. I knew her father. As a child she'd been trained by her aunts to perform in the family's Wild West show, first as a parader and later as a junior sharpshooter of impressive accuracy.

But it was a difficult upbringing, to say the least. A childhood of such turbulence that it could easily have left her broken for life, one of those vague and needy people who depend on others and find no solace, always seeking pity and never finding respect until their eventual unhappy decline. In her case it produced a young woman of early maturity and unusual resilience.

I was unsurprised to hear of her taking on the management of the family's affairs, even when so young. I remember the day she took my hand and read me, to show how easily it could be done.

She was fourteen years old.

SIX

IT WAS a harsh time of year to be travelling. After reassuring Lottie and confiding in Florence, Melody packed a small bag and set out the next morning to board a train for her journey south.

Ever wary of involvement in other people's designs, she'd written and sent a precautionary telegram the evening before. On her arrival in London she emerged from the station to be met under the Euston arch by occasional family employee and gaff lad Alfie Hewitt. In the off season, Alfie worked the markets. Today he was turned out like a boy clerk in a City firm, but one whose suit and bowler had been rescued from the old-clothes pile. Two top buttons held his waistcoat together, under a collar that had never seen starch.

"Wotcher, Melody," he said with a grin.

"Walk with me," she said.

They walked. He offered to carry her bag and she declined.

She said, "Do you remember lifting me a wallet from a gent at the October Fair?"

"Should I?"

She reminded him of the day, and explained what she wanted of him now. "I need you to stay close, stay low, and see where they take me. I never trust these people. You won't have to do anything unless I give you a signal. I just need to be sure that someone knows where I am."

They reached the address she'd been given, just a few streets from the station, and at her word Alfie melted away so that she approached the door alone. It was a shabby hotel with its windows shuttered, overlooking the graveyard behind the Temperance Hospital. After knocking, she had a long wait until the door was opened by a porter in shirtsleeves and carpet slippers. He led her up a dark and dusty stairway to the room where she was to wait. It was sparsely furnished, with just a bare mattress on the bed. She placed her bag on it.

This is no hotel, she thought. She didn't know what it was. But it was no hotel.

The knock on her door came within the hour.

It was Rathbone himself. He said, "Did you unpack?"

"I'm a light traveller."

"There's no bill to cover. Let's go."

There was a car waiting for them outside. A big tourer, carriage-built, with a driver at the wheel and its engine running. Melody felt a moment's anxiety, but London's mix of cars, hand carts and horse traffic would slow them down enough for Alfie to have no trouble keeping the vehicle in sight. Rathbone helped her into the back before climbing in alongside her. The seat was buttoned calfskin, with an expensive rich-leather smell. She sat with her bag on her knees.

They set off, heading south. As they were passing through Bloomsbury, with the driver looking for a chance to pass a removal wagon, Melody said, "How is Lucy?"

Rathbone was looking out of the window. Without turning, he said, "She chose with her heart, and now she's back home."

"I take it she accepted the artist's proposal."

"You remember."

"How did that go?"

"Her father forbade the engagement and they ran away to Paris. The man was true to form and he abandoned her after a month. I had the job of bringing her home and I have to say that for a fallen woman she's showing very little remorse."

Melody passed no comment.

The removal wagon turned off into Russell Square, and a few minutes later they were picking up speed across Waterloo Bridge. Though she took care not to show it, Melody's concern began to grow. Her knowledge of London's geography was mainly tied to the theatres and music halls of her early youth, but it was becoming obvious that their destination was outside the heart of the city, possibly even somewhere out of town. In which case, Alfie Hewitt would have little chance of keeping up. Unless she could find some way to get a message out, those plans for her own security would count for nothing.

By the time they were on the Dover road she knew that she was entirely in the hands of Rathbone and his people, for better or for worse.

AN HOUR into the Kentish countryside, deep in fields whose corners were banked with early snow, they stopped at the gated driveway to a walled estate. By now the hour was late and the daylight all but gone. The driver sounded his horn and a gatekeeper emerged from a cottage just inside the grounds. The driveway beyond ran for two hundred yards or less and the manor house at its end was a minor example of its kind, a square old building with some ill-considered additions.

As they stepped out of the car, she glanced up and saw a figure watching them from a first-floor window.

Aware that he'd been seen, he quickly moved away.

They entered through a modest portico and Melody carried her own bag inside; this time not because she'd refused all offers of help, but because she hadn't received any. The hallway had a black and white stone floor and a glass chandelier, unlit, with illumination from electric fittings on the walls. Somewhere in the building, a telephone was ringing. Rathbone excused himself and disappeared in its direction.

A housekeeper led Melody to the back stairs and up to an attic room, where a fire had been laid but not yet lit. The room was furnished with a bed, a chair, and a washstand where a dinner of bread and cold cuts had been laid out on a covered tray. As the housekeeper crouched before the grate with a lighted taper, Melody looked out of the window. There was little to see now; a vague sense of grounds and gardens, no more.

Pulling the curtains shut, she said, "There was a man at the window downstairs. Is he the one I'm here to see?"

"I really couldn't say," the housekeeper said, rising.

"Do you know his name?"

"No," the housekeeper said, and snuffed out the taper.

Conversation with the staff, it seemed, was not to be encouraged. Moments after the housekeeper had left, Melody heard the turning of a key; and when she tried the door, it had been locked.

She stood for a moment, trying to summon indignation, and then turned away. Her day had been a long one and she was too tired to complain, and the door's simple rim lock would give her very little trouble if she needed to defeat it. So why bother? The fire in the grate was beginning to warm the room, and other than the biscuits she'd brought for on the train she hadn't eaten since breakfast.

It was no way to treat a guest. But this manor was nobody's actual home, she was sure of that. It had the air of those houses commandeered by the military for wartime use, for officer training or to accommodate convalescing troops; the good furniture moved out, rooms repurposed, and the fabric of the building treated with little care. Most such houses were being returned to normal use now that the war was over. This one, clearly not.

After her supper she searched the room for something to read. She found only a Bible in one of the washstand drawers. So she took herself to bed instead.

SEVEN

T HERE WAS a tap on her door the next morning, quite early. By then the fire had burned down to embers and she'd quickly washed in cold water and dressed. When she called out, she heard the key turn. It had been left in the lock overnight, she noted. Rathbone opened the door and looked in.

"You can get breakfast in the kitchen with the servants," he said.

"I'm not a servant."

"Understood. But that's the arrangement. Use the back stairs."

Breakfast was a sombre affair at a long table in a basement kitchen. She ate in the company of the house-keeper, a housemaid, and two men of indeterminate duties. Afterwards she was led across the chandeliered hallway to a drawing-room where she was to meet her subject for the first time.

Rathbone ushered her in. A second man stood looking out of the window, his back to her, framed by faded green velvet curtains that were banded with chintz.

Rathbone said, "This is Melody James. You know why she's here."

The man turned. As she'd expected, it was the figure she'd seen observing her arrival. He was somewhere in his early 'thirties,, fair-haired and slightly freckled, dressed in rugged tweeds and with wire pince-nez spectacles. He wore a pleasant expression, as if this change in his routine was a welcome one.

He moved toward her and held out his hand. She took it.

"Walter Pasmore," he said, and Rathbone made an annoyed sound. With his hand still gripping Melody's, Pasmore looked at Rathbone and said, "What? I'm not allowed a name?"

"We discussed this."

"I know we did, but I should imagine you wouldn't have brought Miss James here if she couldn't be trusted."

"Miss James has an uncle whose fate depends on it," Rathbone said. "So we'd better hope the answer's yes."

Then, to Melody, "Do you need cards?"

"I have cards. If a card reading is what you want."

"I want the same treatment you gave to me," Rathbone said. "But save your conclusions for my ears alone."

A green baize bridge table had been set up with two chairs, away from the window. They took their seats, and Melody produced her much-handled deck. Rathbone seated himself a few feet away.

"I've been looking forward to this," Pasmore said. "Three weeks and they won't even let me see my own newspaper."

Rathbone pointedly cleared his throat, and Melody raised an eyebrow.

Pasmore made a contrite face.

She went through the deck, discarding the low numbers. When she'd finished with the discards, only thirty-six of the high value and court cards were left.

"Well, I'm fascinated," Pasmore said, following her moves with genuine interest.

"I shuffle first," Melody explained. "It removes the

influence of anyone who may have handled the cards before."

She spread them, mixed them, squared up the deck.

"Now you," she said.

"Cut or shuffle?"

"Whichever you prefer."

She pushed the deck to him, and watched as he gave them a simple overhand shuffle.

My own newspaper, he'd said. Hardly a Northcliffe or a Rothermere so . . . a journalist, perhaps.

Socially he was of Rathbone's class, but certainly not of his type. His tweeds were tailored and not cheap but the suit was practical, well lived-in, an obvious favourite. It probably kept his shape when he took it off. The pince-nez gave his appearance a Bohemian touch. His hands had been soft, his grip firm but not aggressive. She noted all these details almost without thinking, adding them to what little she already knew.

Journalist. Traveller. Of use to the government while overseas . . . a foreign correspondent?

She took back the deck and said, "I lay the cards in rows of nine. Each position in the plan has a meaning. The card on that position denotes its meaning for you."

At that point, Rathbone interrupted.

"Can we not have any speaking?" he said.

Both looked at him. "Why not?" Melody said.

"Just do the reading."

Pasmore looked across the table at her. "I think Sir Anthony would like to inject a little scientific rigour into the proceedings," he said.

She smiled and said, "In Sir Anthony's house we play by Sir Anthony's rules."

"Get on with it!"

Pasmore grinned. Melody answered with a faint smile of her own. Sir Anthony's annoyance at their complicity was something for them both to enjoy.

SHE KEPT it going for as long as she could, but it was hard work and it was getting her nowhere. She could spin a lot of spiel out of very little information, but she couldn't pull specifics out of none. Eventually she gathered the cards, sat back from the table, and gestured with open hands.

Finis.

Rathbone went to the door, and called out into the hallway; after a few moments one of the men from her breakfast table appeared and Pasmore was led away.

When Rathbone had closed the door, he turned to Melody and said, "So what did you learn?"

"Nothing," Melody said.

"Nothing?"

"How could I, with no talk and you lurking?"

"What about the cards?"

"The cards are a prop. Everything's a prop. Don't you understand that? You don't read the cards, you read the person. The cards give you a routine to draw them out."

"Then how's this going to work?"

"You have to leave me alone with him for a while."

"No."

"Then make your sceptical friend happy and send me home, because I can't do what you want. How's Walter meant to open up with you perched in the corner waiting to seize on every word?"

"You read me in a minute, and I was giving nothing away."

"You think."

"You have a gift," Rathbone insisted. "I saw it."

"I have knowledge of people. Possibly even more than you."

"I doubt that. You're barely more than a child."

"My father died a wanted criminal," she said. "I had to be rescued from a man who had me a slave to morphine by the time I was fourteen. On my twenty-first birthday I inherited the family business. I cashed in the act and now I manage four rides and three portables and when my aunt got married I threw her a wedding with four hundred show people from all over the country. You want me to look into a man's soul, I can do that for you. But not with tricks."

There was a silence. Then:

"I'll need to know everything he tells you," Rathbone said.

EIGHT

THOUGH SHE'D told him the plain truth, Melody knew that Rathbone would quite likely persist in thinking that her 'gift' was real. She'd seen this many times before. Mediums who admitted to fraud would have their confessions dismissed by the faithful with too much invested to roll back their beliefs. *It's the spirits who move you,* they'd insist. *Why do you try so hard to deny it? How can you be so blind?*

The afternoon session took place in the same drawing-room, this time with the two of them alone. It was a development that surprised Walter Pasmore.

"Where's our host?" he said.

"I gave him permission to leave us alone."

"How did he take that?"

"He's gone, hasn't he?"

Pasmore considered that, nodded, looked around, and seemed at a loss for a response to this unexpected lifting of supervision. He said, "And now what?"

"I'm supposed to use my psychic powers to tell him if you can be trusted."

"Psychic powers."

"I don't have any."

"Good on you. How much are you getting for this?"

"If it goes well, my useless uncle won't get beaten to death in prison."

"Families," he sympathised.

She gave a little shrug, as if to say, *What can you do?*

Pasmore said, "Will you tell him what he's looking to

hear? That's how it works, isn't it?"

"I won't do that. I'll do my best to give him the truth. We didn't exactly spit and shake, but deal's a deal."

"Then tell me how I can help with this uncle of yours."

"Talk to me," she said. "What's all this for?"

He said, "I'm a journalist by trade. For the past three years I've been the Star Tribune's correspondent in Petrograd. They want to use my contacts amongst the Bolsheviks to gather intelligence that will help the White movement. You know what that means?"

"I do."

"I have a reputation out there as a trusted witness."

"And that could go."

"If I was ever found out, yes it would. I lived through a revolution with those people. I gave a fair report on their cause when it suited others to dismiss them. They'll talk to me like they'll talk to no other."

They moved to sit by the window, and he told her his story.

"I WAS MEDICALLY unfit for war service and hadn't the experience to land a war correspondent's job, but there was an English family I could stay with in Petrograd. So I went out via Sweden and for two years I was picking up news from the Eastern front and sending my articles to an agent in London. When the Tribune's correspondent fell ill, I had enough language and local knowledge to be recommended for the job."

A stream of articles and reportage had followed. Much of it first-hand, some of it culled from the Russian press. The contacts that he'd made during the war years now gave him unprecedented access to those involved in the fall of Kerensky's provisional government and the subsequent Bolshevik coup, the so-called October Revolution. His output was read with growing anxiety back home; among the princes and politicians of Europe there was a growing fear that the people's revolt might catch on and spread.

Nervous governments were looking for ways to give indirect help to any counter-revolutionary movement. London offered shelter to White Russian exiles and such portable treasure as they could run with. Beyond that, any meaningful support was problematical; while the Bolshevik Reds were united around a cause, the Whites stood for no specific thing other than the clawing back of their privilege.

"History's never kind to its *réactionnaires*," Pasmore explained. "Jewellery and property's of no help when you're being strung up or shot. And I can't say some of them won't have asked for it."

For the past few minutes he'd been on his feet and walking around as he talked, gazing at remembered landscapes, moving and reliving his past as he described it. Now, standing by the window, he took a moment to think. "I probably shouldn't have said that." He turned and looked accusingly at Melody. "You're too easy to talk to, Miss James."

"I'm not here to cause you trouble," she said.

"Do people always share their confidences with you?"

"I tend to find that they do."

He considered this for a moment, and then went on to wrap up his story.

On his return to England he was brought to this house to be questioned as a suspected Bolshevik sympathiser, which he insisted he was not.

Now Rathbone and his people wanted to use Pasmore's hard-won position of trust for their own purposes. They wished him to return and continue his work as a journalist while being a carrier of covert messages and a point of contact for their agents. On the face of it an impartial observer, in reality an instrument in their mission to undermine the Reds.

"And they won't let you leave until you agree?"

"They're very determined."

"I have to tell them something," Melody said. "What would you want me to say?"

"If you want to give them the truth," Pasmore said, "tell them I love my friends as much as I love my country. It's not right to make me choose."

AT THE END of the session, Pasmore was led away again and Rathbone stayed to speak. He closed the door and said, "What's the verdict?"

Melody sat with her hands folded on her lap. "I say he's a decent man," she said. "A dreamer, for sure. His sympathy for the Reds is more sentimental than logical, but it's real. If he says he'll help you, then I think you can be certain he means it. But any promise he makes to you now could be undone by some greater influence once he's back over there."

"That's not as much as I was hoping for."

"Only because you want him to commit to something he doesn't believe in."

Rathbone shook his head. "The case for supporting the Whites is a strong one. I've laid it all out for him."

"I don't think you believe in it either."

"I believe in the necessity of it."

"Not the same thing."

"Three months ago his beloved Reds murdered their own royal family in a cellar. And that included the children. Did he mention that?"

"No."

"No," Rathbone said, "I'm sure. If it could happen to the Tsar it could happen to the King. Make him see that."

"That's not what you asked of me."

"I'm asking it now."

"Three days, you said."

"I said three days ought to do it. There's still a way to go. Unless you'd rather leave your uncle to his fate."

"That's unfair."

"You drove the bargain but if I have to modify the terms, I will. You have no idea how hard this job can be. I have to compel people to fidelity while I school them in betrayal."

"If I stay," Melody said, "I'm not to be locked in my room."

"I'll have a word with the staff."

Later that evening, with her dinner finished and the tray taken away, she once again heard the soft click of the key being turned in the door.

NINE

SIR ANTHONY Gair Rathbone came down to the basement kitchen during breakfast the next morning, causing instant unease and an awkward atmosphere amongst the staff around the table. With a motion of his head, he indicated for Melody to step out with him. In the limewashed corridor between the kitchen and the butler's pantry he said, "Pasmore's being obstinate today. He wants to get out of the house this morning. He wants to walk in the grounds."

"I know how he feels. Can we do that?"

"Do you think it will help?"

"It might."

"It takes at least three men to watch him. I only have two."

"I'll watch him for you," she said. "I want this to be over."

The morning was clear and crisp, with days-old snow on the manor grounds lying patchy and undisturbed. Melody bundled up in all her layers, and the house-keeper found her a shawl for extra warmth. When Pasmore was brought out, she saw that he was in his regular tweeds but he'd added a scarf and a favourite hat.

Pasmore's escort moved to a polite distance, but it was clear that their walk was to be supervised. In a low voice Pasmore said, "How did Sir Anthony take your report?"

"Yesterday I had to read your character for him.

Today I'm supposed to persuade you."

"There's no end to it, then."

"At some point they'll give up."

"Or I'll give in. Shall we?"

Beyond the garden there was an orchard, leafless and orderly. Beyond the orchard, a neglected coppice. The air around them had a pure, blue-water clarity as they set out from the house. Wherever it hadn't cleared, the leftover snow had frozen into a thin, hard layer that broke underfoot.

Melody said, "Where are they keeping you?"

"First floor up, the room where you saw me that first night. You?"

"Up the back stairs in the attic. No bars but they lock the door on me."

Melody glanced back. The gatehouse keeper had been drafted in to serve as third watchman. The guards kept their distance, but moved along with them. They made lonely figures, hands thrust into their overcoat pockets, their faces pinched and cold. Should Pasmore launch off in any direction, one or other of them would be well-placed to intercept him.

He said, "A locked door would be no great obstacle to you carnival folk, I'm sure. Are you with a carnival or circus? Or the music hall, perhaps?"

"Fairgrounds. We had a Wild West act but I wound it up. My aunts didn't want to perform and my uncle . . ."

"The useless one?"

"You don't get to call him that."

He took the rebuke. "Forgive me."

She said, "Ours is a family business. Someone had to take it on."

"You're very young."

"Don't start."

Much like the house, these gardens were superficially tidy but lacked any sign of ownerly pride or loving care. As they moved through the orchard, she saw that fruit had been left to rot on the branch at the season's end. Someone had lived here once, and called it their own; hung their pictures, laid out the grounds, greeted their friends at the door. Now it was a place of caretakers. All who passed through were strangers on business with little concern for their surroundings.

She said, "The car came back last night. I heard the engine but I couldn't see who was in it."

"That was Oswald Grenville. He's something in the government. He stayed less than an hour."

"Was he here to speak to you?"

"No, he was with Sir Anthony the whole time. My room's right above the library but I couldn't make out anything of what they were saying."

They walked on for a while and then Pasmore threw his head back and took a deep, appreciative breath of the cold air.

He said, "This is the first time I've been out in a week. They keep me comfortable but I have no freedom. They need my willing co-operation so they're wearing me down."

"How did they get you here?"

"I was arrested," he said, "when I came back to England on private family business. Someone followed me down from the boat at Newcastle and they picked me up at King's Cross."

"So you really are a prisoner?"

"They're calling me a guest."

Despite Rathbone's instructions, Melody had no

argument to offer him in support of the spymaster's case. The choice was his alone to make. She said as much.

"But if he asks," she said, "will you tell him I tried?"

Pasmore said he understood; that she found herself pressed into an unpleasant job toward an end that she didn't believe in.

"Your situation is not unlike my own," he said.

The orchard ended and the coppice began. There was a path, of sorts, winding through the trees. They walked on frozen twigs and dead bracken.

He said, "When the River Neva freezes, the covering is more than two feet thick. The Empress Anna had blocks of it cut to build an entire palace on the bank. The palace had furniture, statues, and working cannon to guard the doors. All carved from the ice. Imagine that, lit up at night."

"She'd make a good showman."

"It was built to torture a prince for the crime of falling in love," he said. "The Empress staged a mock wedding and locked the couple in naked for their wedding night. The bride caught pneumonia and was dead in a week."

"Ah."

"The revolution was a long time coming."

Out beyond the coppice, a hedgerow marked the boundary of the estate with a lane and fields beyond. The hedgerow was long-established, a ragged mix of hawthorn and bramble and thick-rooted trees. Melody paused by one specimen with a double trunk and laid a hand against its bark, to stand for a moment in thoughtful silence before moving on.

He watched as she stood, and said nothing.

She asked him about his own life in Russia. He told

her of his tiny Petrograd apartment, of the Russian poetry he translated for pleasure, of the obstinacy of British officials in Russian dealings. He quoted some of the poetry in the original, and apologised for his pronunciation. His affection for the country and its ordinary people seemed deep and sincere.

And after a while he said, "I have to ask. How old was the child you lost?"

The question startled her.

"I beg your pardon?"

"You stopped by those twin oaks. I've been told that when gypsies bury a child they lay it to rest with an acorn in each hand. So to someone in the know, the sight of twin oaks can suggest a baby's grave."

"I'm no gypsy."

"I misread your thoughts," he said, and, once again: "Forgive me."

They walked on, and for a while neither spoke.

Here was a green pond, with a neglected pergola running beside it for a dozen feet or less. An archway of trelliswork, wound through with climbing roses and ivy. Pasmore seemed to grow tense as they approached it. Melody was aware of the shift in his mood, and was immediately on her guard.

He said, "Would you do something for me?"

"That depends," Melody said.

"I need to get a letter out," he said. "I can swear to you that it's a personal matter, nothing to do with their politics. If you'll promise to deliver it, I'll agree right now to whatever they're asking. They'll be happy and you can go home."

"What makes you think you can trust me?"

"If I can't trust the one decent person I've met in this

whole sorry affair, then it's not worth my going on. Please."

It was obvious that he'd planned this. They were close to the end of their walk. As they passed through the pergola they'd be out of anyone's sight for, at most, two or three steps, time enough to pass the correspondence. But it had to be smooth and continuous, a conjuror's move. Any hesitation or break in pace would betray the trick.

They passed under the trellis.

She took the letter.

When they emerged from the arbour, the paper that had been secreted in Pasmore's coat was now hidden in Melody's clothing. Their watchers seemed unperturbed, each most likely assuming that the others had the moment covered.

"There's no address," she said.

"I'll tell you the address. No one else is to know it."

She repeated the details back to him. Words spoken aloud lodged best in the memory, she'd always found. The house was ahead of them now. She wondered if Rathbone might be watching from a window. If Pasmore was true to his word, then this meeting would be their last.

"My husband was Roma," Melody said. "Our child didn't survive the birth."

Pasmore took a moment to appreciate the gravity of this revelation, and then said, "I'm sorry. You're a widow?"

"It was a broomstick marriage and it lasted less than a year. He raised his hand to me, just the once. When the drink wore off he woke to the edge of my knife tickling his hamstring. He was a juggler and balancer."

"So he feared for his living."

"His choice was to get out, or never to sleep in peace again. He was last heard of in Lincolnshire, not that I have any interest. He was so handsome and I was infatuated, for a while." She added, "I have a history of weakness in such matters."

"You don't strike me as weak."

"We're all weak somewhere. The trick to being strong is in how you hide it."

A RAMSHACKLE SHED marked the start of the kitchen garden. They made small talk all the way to the manor's side entrance, where they once again went their separate ways; she with her housekeeper, he with his guards.

She was led to the library, the room that Rathbone had co-opted as his office for the duration of his stay. It had a large leather-topped desk on which stood the house telephone. Behind him were rows of books shelved floor to ceiling, great tomes bound in uniform leather. Old books that came with the property; county records, statutes of the land, and the obligatory classics in the original Greek.

Rathbone broke off in the middle of whatever he was writing, looked up under his brows, and said, "Well?"

"He's minded to cooperate."

Rathbone laid down his pen and sat back. "What changed his opinion?"

"Your story of those executions," she lied. "He's sensitive to the deaths of children."

Rathbone considered this, and seemed to find it plausible.

She went on, "He says he'll do whatever you ask. But if you want my honest reading of him, he'll never really be your man. He'll be sincere in his intentions but at some point his heart will take over."

"Sincere but unreliable? That's your reading?"

She looked pointedly at Rathbone. She said, "We all know someone who'll promise one thing and then feel compelled to modify the terms."

Rathbone turned in his chair so that he could get a hand into his pocket.

"Hold out your hand," he said.

She complied. He reached across the desk and dropped three pennies into her outstretched palm.

"Trust me now?" he said.

She examined them. The coins all bore the late Queen's head. Sweated coins were made by shaving two pennies and then bonding the halves to make one coin of uneven balance. These were well made, but one had a date on the reverse that couldn't possibly be right, unless the old Queen had briefly risen from the dead.

Melody sighed.

"Oh, Jack," she said sorrowfully.

"You now hold the prosecution's evidence, and your uncle has his liberty."

"Then I can go home," she said.

He picked up his pen once more.

"Perhaps tomorrow," he said, and she was dismissed.

TEN

MELODY DIDN'T much like the sound of that 'perhaps'. Alone in her room that evening, away from both the window and the door, she took out Pasmore's secret letter and examined it. It was a plain sheet of paper with no envelope, folded and sealed with a drop of candle wax. The paper had one ragged edge. They no doubt supervised his access to writing materials but if each room had a Bible like her own, he'd most likely torn out a flyleaf to compose his message on.

She unsealed the paper and looked at the note, but found it to be in the Russian language with no more than a few characters and numerals that were comprehensible to her. After a few minutes' study she warmed the wax at her fire and resealed it.

Then she lay fully clothed on her bed, listening to the house as it settled through the evening.

Sometime after midnight she took the slender butter knife that she'd kept back from her supper. Crouching at her door, she carefully jiggled and poked the key out of its keyhole so that it fell to the floor outside. From there she could use the same instrument to hook it in through the gap.

The sound of its fall could easily have been mistaken for one of the creaks and cracks of a building's timbers at night. Nevertheless, she waited a good ten minutes before easing the lock and venturing out.

She'd memorised her way in the dark, and she knew how to be light on her feet. For added certainty she walked in her stockings and carried her shoes. By these actions she'd no doubt be forfeiting the unpaid fee. But with the evidence against Jack safe in her possession, she already had what she needed from the deal.

If Rathbone meant to let her go, nothing was lost by an early departure. And if he did not . . . then twenty pounds would have to be the price of her liberty.

She negotiated the stairs without noise or mishap. By far the longest part of her escape was spent loosening and sliding the two bolts on the door to the kitchen garden. Every other exit that she'd seen had a deadlock, and the ground floor windows were screwed shut, so this was her only option.

With the bolts drawn, she lifted the thumb-latch with her fingers. There was no way to avoid the sound of its fall if she were to close the door behind her. So she left the door ajar.

There were clouds but there was also a moon, and the frosty crust on the ground reflected some of its light. The effect was almost theatrical. She took aim across the kitchen garden, making for the ink-blue shadows of the wooden building at its end.

During that morning's walk, she'd picked out several places where a person might escape the grounds without passing the gates or the keeper's cottage. Nothing looked quite the same in the dark, however. Further care was required.

"Wotcher, Melody," came a voice right by her ear.

ELEVEN

MELODY WAS not one for screaming. In this moment she might have made an exception, had the breath not been shocked from her. A hand quickly steadied her elbow, lest she fall.

"*Alfie?*" she said when she had sufficiently recovered. "How did you find me?"

"Didn't need to," Alfie whispered. "Stole a bicycle and followed the car like a regular Sexton Blake."

For a moment she didn't know whether to curse him or bless him. When her heart had settled to a normal rhythm they moved away from the house and out toward the orchard, to be completely sure that they wouldn't be overheard.

Alfie had been there from the beginning, sleeping under sacks in the kitchen garden shed, watching the house through its cobwebbed windows, relieving himself in the orchard and living off kitchen scraps that put many a slop house to shame. Where there was snow, he walked in the tracks of others. All of this, without ever attracting the notice of anyone in the manor. He'd crept out to forage food from the pig bin when he saw her emerge.

She said, "I need the bicycle. Can you make your way back without it?"

Alfie had no doubt that he could. He seemed barely affected by his ordeal, to the extent that he seemed to think it no ordeal at all.

"I'll show you my way out to the lane," he said.

They retrieved the bicycle from its hiding place in a ditch. She gave Alfie a guinea with the promise of much more, and set off down the lane by moonlight.

These were not good roads, and she steered with care. When the lane passed under a railway bridge, she took the next turn and followed the line through silent countryside. She cycled past empty fields of hop poles, long rows of empty huts for seasonal pickers.

By the time she found a station, the first light of dawn was beginning to show in the sky. The station was on a high bank, reached by a flight of wooden steps. Melody lifted the bicycle over a hedge and abandoned it there, heading up to the platform to await the first London train. I would love to tell you that she felt a pang of conscience for its deprived owner, whose very livelihood might have depended on its use. But we would both know better than that.

The station was on a two-track branch line with a wooden footbridge and one waiting room. The waiting room offered all-night heat from a small iron stove. She sat alone by it for some time, and as the dawn took hold a few other early travellers appeared. None showed any interest in her, or in each other.

When the booking office opened she bought a third-class ticket to Charing Cross from a man in a stiff collar who appeared to serve as station master, porter, and signalman all in one.

Five people boarded the first London train of the day. Melody was one of them.

TWELVE

MELODY JAMES would keep her word, but she was far from naïve. She didn't know what Walter Pasmore's letter contained, or for whose eyes it was ultimately intended; for all that she did know, she could be participating in a dangerous act of treason. For that reason if no other, she would proceed with care.

By mid-morning she was making her way to Kensington. At the address that she'd memorised stood the Worcester House private hotel, on the corner of Cromwell Road and Courtfield Gardens. A modest *pension* compared to the likes of the Metropole, with rates for weekly boarders. She had the option of leaving the note at the door, but remembering Pasmore's urging—deliver by hand, and in person—she chose to take it to the suite.

Her knock was answered quickly by a young woman around her own age. Dark-eyed, snub-nosed, short-haired, and apprehensive. She seemed disappointed to see Melody.

Melody said, "I'm looking for Valya."

"My sister is Valya," the young woman said. "I'm Zhenya."

"I have news from Walter Pasmore."

The young woman all but closed the door on her, leaving Melody to contemplate Zhenya's knuckles gripping the woodwork as a hurried conversation took place on the other side. After a few moments, the door was opened wide and she was beckoned in.

She'd been wrong to imagine a suite. This had to be the smallest and most economical bedroom in the hotel. The furniture left little floor space, and the bed was their couch. Wherever she looked, the sisters' clothes were spread out to air or to dry.

The second sister was older and more heavy-set, but the family resemblance was there. Melody said to her, "Walter gave me this address. I have a letter for you."

It seemed that Valya spoke no English. Zhenya translated for her, and Melody saw distress and relief as the words were relayed. She held out the paper with its candlewax seal.

Zhenya said, "We've been here a month with no money. When is Walter coming for us?"

"I don't know," Melody said, "and I can't stay to explain. Read the letter."

"She needs her husband."

Understanding dawned. As Valya sat on the bed and fumbled open the paper Melody said, "Does anyone else know you're here?"

"Please God, no," Zhenya said.

"Then what was the plan?"

The story can be quickly told. Valya, short for Valentina, had been Walter Pasmore's reader and researcher in Petrograd, finding stories in the Russian press that he could use for his articles. They'd married in secret, and he'd managed to secure her a German passport to get her across neutral borders to England. Having fled her Bolshevik homeland, she could never return. Nor could Yevgeniya—Zhenya—the loyal sister who'd volunteered to accompany her. The plan was for them to wait here for Walter to join them, but he'd yet to appear.

As Zhenya was explaining this, Valya was reading. She looked up and there was an exchange of words, after which Zhenya turned to Melody.

"Walter needs us to stay hidden," she said. "Why?"

None of this was her problem, and nor did she wish it to be. Yet here she was.

"There were unexpected difficulties," Melody said.

"What are we to do?"

She looked at the two of them, two lost, scared, and penniless young women in a land where they'd find little welcome, and said, "I know some Russian families. Let me tell them where to find you."

"That's not what he wants."

"But it may be the safest way."

At that moment, there was a light tapping at the door.

Valya was on her feet. "*Walter!*" she said.

Zhenya rushed to answer the knock.

Sir Anthony Gair Rathbone stood in the doorway, with several uniformed police officers in the passageway behind him.

"Thank you, Miss James," he said. "That's all we need from you."

And then, to a man at his shoulder, "Take her downstairs and wait for me."

THIRTEEN

"THIS IS what you intended," she said.

"We knew he had a wife. Just not where he'd stashed her."

The private hotel had few facilities, but a small dining room was one of them. Melody had waited in the company of the constable assigned to watch her. He had done so with arms folded and a steady, unnerving, unblinking gaze across the table. He didn't speak, other than to tell her to sit down and stay quiet while outside a curious crowd gathered. On the nearby stairs there was much coming and going and eventually she saw the two Russian sisters pass the dining room on their way to a waiting car. Two policewomen were escorting them and none of the party glanced her way.

Rathbone came down a few minutes later, and took the constable's place.

Melody asked him, "Was I followed?"

"Of course you were followed. We didn't expect the bicycle, but we picked you up at the station."

"A lot of men, for just two frightened women."

"We didn't know what we'd find. Could have been a nest of revolutionaries all ready to shoot their way out."

"What now?"

"We'll give them a few days together. Then we'll take care of the women while Pasmore returns to Russia. He'll do valuable work for his country with no danger of any change of heart."

"I was used."

"You played your part. And take care what you say after this. What was done for your uncle Jack can easily be undone."

"I've no fears for Jack. He'll have vanished the moment he stepped out of the gates. If the Brugnetti brothers can't find him then the police have no chance."

She leaned forward. "Tell me something," she said. "Was it a sham from the start? Did you ever really want my reading of Walter's character?"

"I needed you to be plausible, Miss James," Rathbone said. "And you are an exceptional performer."

"That's how you sold it to your friend Oswald, I'm sure. But I've seen you shaken. I think there's still a part of you that believes in higher forces. You can't help it."

"Are you reading me now?" he said. "Don't over-estimate your gift. You told me yourself, you need information to work with. I expect you had some advance knowledge to use against me."

"You know that? Or you're guessing?"

"It's the logical explanation," he said. "What are you doing?"

She'd set her pasteboard deck on the table before him.

"Cut the cards," she said.

"I don't think so."

She waited.

He shook his head and looked at the ceiling.

Still she waited.

Then he shrugged, and with his left hand he made the cut.

Melody quickly dealt, discarded, organised, arranged the deck. Rathbone cast an uneasy glance toward the open doorway, mindful of how it might look—the boss, having his fortune told. He adopted a tolerant manner, a display of wry patience. Indulge the child, let her do what she must. But he didn't tell her to stop.

"I see success," she said. "Rising to fame. Great honour."

His manner didn't change, but his eyes followed the cards.

"Choose your fortune card and turn it," she said.

"I don't think I'll—"

"Choose and turn."

Like his niece long before him, he hovered. Then he seemed to grow annoyed with himself, and quickly turned over the nearest of the two discards. It was the King of Diamonds.

"King of Diamonds," he said. "Does that mean wealth?"

"Disgrace. Sorry."

"How does a King mean disgrace?"

"Don't take it too seriously," Melody said. "It's all just in fun."

She gathered the deck, leaving the King on the table. "Keep the card," she said. "A memento of your big day."

"I don't think so," he said, and pushed it back toward her. "No hard feelings?"

"Who would that profit?" she said. "Now can I go?"

He spread his hands as if to say, no one's preventing you.

She returned the King of Diamonds to her deck, gave him a polite nod, and gathered her belongings to leave.

FOURTEEN

I T MIGHT have ended there. But it did not.

Melody James returned to the family's winter quarters. She sold the ghost show, took a part share in a bricks-and-mortar Picture Palace in Chester, and had the travelling business back on the road in time for the King's Lynn charter fair the next spring. The Brugnetti brothers were sent to trial, both of them on charges of aggravated assault. One served three months in Preston gaol while the other received a longer sentence and served it in Strangeways Prison. Jack was released by the Blackpool magistrates' court and never resurfaced, at least not under his own name. If the James family knew where he was, they weren't saying.

Within a year, the *Manchester Guardian* carried a report that British journalist Walter Pasmore had been driven to woodland near Vibetsk and executed with a single shot, with suspicion falling upon agents of the Commission for Combating Counter-Revolution. The Bolshevik administration denied any knowledge of his fate and no body was ever found.

There was no record of what happened to Valya and Zhenya, nor have I been able to unearth any.

Melody's forecast of good fortune for Sir Anthony Gair Rathbone was not entirely inaccurate. He did, indeed, gain a promotion and a knighthood, mainly for the intelligence work in wartime that was a matter of public record. But his life was about to take an unpleasant turn.

Some time after the newspaper reports of Pasmore's death I received an unusual summons.

Until the hostilities I'd served as an investigator for the Lord Chancellor's Visitor in Lunacy, but during the war years I played a part in Military Intelligence. Rathbone had been my distant superior. The message summoned me to the Great Marlborough Street police station where Sir Anthony was being held.

My first reaction was that they must have the wrong man. Sir Anthony? It surely couldn't be. But he'd been detained earlier that evening in Hyde Park after being discovered in the company of a young woman whom he now claimed not to know. Both were found with their clothing in disarray, and when questioned he was unable to give an account of himself. The young woman had been bailed and released, but Sir Anthony was proving, as they described it, 'something of a handful'.

"Are you absolutely sure it's him?" I said, but the messenger could only shrug at the unlikelihood of it. Many a policeman would know Sir Anthony on sight; he'd clashed with so many of them over the years. His methods had made him few friends in the Met, and I imagined he could expect no favours now.

A charge of lewd behaviour seemed unavoidable. Such a prominent figure demanded careful handling, and the duty officers didn't know what to do with him. His answers were rambling and vague, and he seemed uncertain as to how he'd got himself into this situation. In the space of an hour he'd given three different versions of events.

So they cast around for help, and landed upon me. Where I'd first assumed that they were calling on me for my wartime connection, I had in fact been recommended because of my previous experience with the eminent insane. My Chancery job, whenever the question arose, had been to determine whether those in possession of a fortune were fit to manage it. Not to diagnose madness, that was a doctor's task. Mine was to expose the strategies they or their families might use to avoid the legal process.

Someone clearly thought that Rathbone's alarming behaviour warranted those skills.

He was not so alarming when I got to him. I was let into the room where he was being held, and his face seemed to light up at the sight of me.

"Becker," he said. "Becker, my old friend! Can you get me out of this? I'll give anything."

We were not old friends. I don't think we'd been in the same room more than three or four times before that night. He offered his hand and I took it; though the room was warm, I noted that his grip was cool and clammy.

"Anything," he repeated.

"Good evening, Sir Anthony," I said. "I'm sorry that we're meeting again in such circumstances. Can you explain to me how you come to be here?"

"A tragic misunderstanding," he said. "Make them see it," he added, "or it'll be the ruin of me."

His hair was awry, his stiff collar sprung. He seemed diminished, distracted. I could smell no drink on him, and as far as I was aware he remained a sworn tee-totaller. Yet the word in the building was that he was surely intoxicated. I began to look for other causes. By this time I saw no signs of the euphoria they'd described to me. Rather, he seemed weary. When he finally released my hand, he slumped back in his chair.

I said, "They tell me you tried to bribe the officer who arrested you. That's a serious charge."

He shook his head. "Never happened," he said.

"What *did* happen?"

He shook his head slowly, and so steadily and for so long that I began to think I wasn't going to get an answer.

"I actually can't remember," he said.

"It was no more than a few hours ago."

"I know."

He looked at me then, helpless. It was startling. His pupils were like tiny flyspecks, giving his ordinarily blue eyes an almost inhuman character. It was an effect that I'd seen before in the course of my work. It generally betrayed those who'd been using morphine, or had been doped with it.

"Sir Anthony," I said. "Are you by any chance under a doctor's care?"

"Me?" he said, and he made a fist and thumped his chest. "Healthy as a horse." Then he beckoned me forward, and leaned in as if to impart a confidence.

"Melody James!" he said in a fierce whisper. "She knows. She knows everything."

Melody James.

I could get nothing more from him that night. I reported my observations to the police and took my leave. By that time Sir Anthony was fast asleep in his chair, head flung back, snoring like a hog.

By the next morning Sir Anthony was himself again, but it was too late. He appeared in the dock, protested his innocence, and was fined five pounds. There was laughter in the court as the charges were read. The penalty for his offence was light, but his career was over.

I asked, but I never got to see the young woman from the park. Her two-pound fine was paid by a man who described himself as a press photographer. Those who saw him described him as thick-set, sandy-haired, with a drinker's complexion. He carried no camera.

When they spoke of her it was of the fairness of her skin, the lightness of her air-blue gown. Afterwards the two of them disappeared together. The name she'd given was almost certainly a fiction.

While putting together this narrative I had sight of the police ledger for that night. The account of Sir Anthony's arrest was meticulously detailed, right down to the picture in his wallet and the contents of his pockets.

Amongst his effects recorded by the custody sergeant was a single playing card, of a number and suit they failed to note.

I've no idea what happened to it.

.

Stephen Gallagher is the author of fifteen novels including Valley of Lights, the Boat House, and The Spirit Box. For a glimpse of Melody's early life, read on for a sample section and chapter from **The Authentic William James**.

THE TESTAMENT OF WILLIAM JAMES (1)

NINETEEN

L ET ME first say how much I regret deceiving you. Out of all who dealt with me, your behaviour was the closest to any form of kindness. My actions have been a poor form of repayment but when you have read the words that I am about to set down, I believe you will understand what lay behind them.

I care nothing for what happens to me. My sole concern is for the fate of my daughter Melody James. Though Kit Strong has managed to extinguish in her any love or loyalty she may have felt for her father, mine for her remains undimmed. Such, I suppose, is the instinct of the human animal.

This is much harder than I imagined it would be.

Where did it really begin? When I took her out of Liverpool, I imagine. I removed her from friends and the only home she knew for a life on the road, an only child among adults. But my father was dead and his legacy was there, demanding that I take it up. I had little enough to show for my own efforts; no wife, no savings, and a few possessions in two rented rooms on Parliament Street. There was also the livelihood of my bereaved mother and my sisters to consider. I looked into the possibility of selling the show and dividing the spoils, but the paper value of the assets was negligible. If I knew one thing well, it was bookkeeping. Our family's fortune lay in costumes, weapons, wagons, some practised skills, and a book of dates. All of these added up to this one great intangible, a thing of value but with no material substance—the Act.

I began by writing to the managers at all our bookings, assuring them that dates would be kept and obligations met. Florence set about altering my father's wardrobe to fit me, and I began to practice those skills I'd tried hard to forget. My father's patter was fixed in my memory still; I would rely on it, having little talent for improvisation of my own.

Then there was the matter of the name. I could have continued as The One and Only Bronco Billy James. But after giving up everything else to be drawn back in, I was unwilling to disappear completely into my father's shadow. I sized up the lettering on the wagons and the banner and settled upon The Authentic William James, a change that would incur the least expense with the sign painter.

Melody took to the life, in a way that both relieved and depressed me. Relief of course, for who does not want their child to be happy? But the rapport she found with her aunts and with the vague, extended and ever-fluid family of show folk was something that I envied. She and I had never been as close. She got on well with Lottie and Jack, and Florence had a breezy charmer of a husband at that time, a ride operator on the steam yachts. His name was Frank Leatherbarrow. Melody would help on the ride and he'd let her pick up the change that fell from customers' pockets.

It was Florence who persuaded me to let Melody dress as an Indian Squaw and join the act as a parader, and it was Florence who began teaching her how to use a rifle.

"I don't know, Florence," I said. "She wasn't born to this."

"None of us was, William," Florence said to me, "but we took to it when we had to. She'll not thank you for denying her a part."

The husband didn't last but the rifle lessons did, and we adapted the act to give Melody a spot where she'd shoot out a balloon that we'd filled with confetti. It was a good effect, and a cheap one to achieve. Florence said, "She's got a good eye and a steady nerve. She's one of us, all right."

It was not enough. On the fairgrounds we got by, but on theatrical dates our weaknesses were exposed. Other Western acts offered more, from a horse thief lynching to complete two-act dramas with scenery. Jack set out to write us a sketch but managed no more than two pages, which was two pages more than the playwright who took my money and produced nothing.

When a captive audience grows restless, there's no mistaking it. One manager's words stung me when paying us off at the end of the engagement; "Not so wild, this Wild West of yours, is it now?" he said.

He was right. For a bunch of cowboys, we were not very dangerous. All the whooping and hollering couldn't disguise the fact that the heart had gone out of the act. My father could split a playing card in your hand with a bullwhip, shoot a pipe out of your mouth while looking over his shoulder in a mirror, outline a human target with his giant knives. What could I do? I could repeat his patter. I could draw fast and spin guns in both hands. I could even shatter a glass ball in mid-air, with a little bit of cheating. But Jack couldn't be trusted with a human target, and I could not enthral the public as my father once had. That's a gift, and I don't have it. Florence was our major talent now, but she could not carry us all.

My aim in business was to get us onto the books of one of the major variety circuits. At this rate, it wasn't going to happen. After my failure in securing a play I tried various other strategies, but it was only when I heard of Kit Strong that I believed I might have found our missing element.

I interviewed Strong at the Holborn Empire and came away with mixed feelings. At the time he was making his living in the wrestling ring, a fighter in tights and a headband, but if he possessed half of the skills that he claimed I could see him being a valuable asset to our company. Given his circumstances, I'd hoped to get him cheap. In that I was disappointed.

He joined us a few weeks later, and we set about reshaping the act. Because of a leg shortened in an accident, he couldn't handle some of the rope tricks that had once been part of his repertoire. His accuracy with a pistol had never left him—he brought his own guns, a pair of well-used and workmanlike Colts—but he was no longer able to spin a rope and step in and out of it with the grace he once had. He could pull the arm bounces and rolls, the thrown loops and catches. But the Texas skip and the crow step, the spoke jump and the butterfly—all were off the menu.

He said to me, "You seem disappointed. You

wanted more roping?" It was a Saturday morning and we were running through some routines away from the public's gaze, in the yard of a pub in Islington.

I said, "That was the hope I had. Until I knew the extent of your problem with the leg."

"Problems are there to be beaten," Kit Strong said. "Can you fetch your daughter?"

"For what?"

"A demonstration. An experiment. Whatever you want to call it."

I sent for her. Kit Strong was coiling the rope in his hands as she came over.

He said, "Hello, Melody." I don't believe they'd ever addressed each other directly before this.

"Mr Strong," she said.

"Did you ever play jump rope, Melody? I'm guessing that you have. I never knew a little girl who didn't."

Melody looked to me, confused.

"He means have you ever played with a skipping rope," I said.

Melody said, "I have, sir."

Strong held up the coil for her to see. "The *vaqueros* call this a lariat," he said. "The rubes call it a lasso. I just call it a rope. See this metal runner? That gives a little weight to the spin so I can do this."

He took a step back from her to give himself some room, and began to spin the line. In his hands looked easy, almost effortless, as if the rope itself had taken life and was doing the actual work.

As he worked it he kept up a commentary, saying, "You've seen me do this. The flat loop. This here's the merry-go-round. And this one's called the wedding ring. Okay, Melody. Come and stand close. Face me now."

She did as instructed. I could sense rest of the family gathering behind me to watch.

The loop was spinning over their heads, describing a perfect circle in the air. Strong said, "I'm going to bring the loop almost down to the ground between us. When I say now, you skip over it."

He kept his roping arm high above his head, and the loop descended around Strong, encircling him. This was the move that he'd called the wedding ring. As he accelerated the spin, the loop grew larger.

"Now," he said.

Melody was short enough to skip inside the loop without fouling it. Now they were both inside the ring. They were only inches apart and Florence and Lottie clapped for encouragement.

Then Melody tried to skip out on his cue, but her feet tangled with the rope and it all went wrong.

"I don't think so," I began, but Melody said, "Let me try again."

Kit Strong said, "Why don't you leave us be for a while. I'll call you when there's something to see."

That was where it really began.

They perfected the wedding ring, and went on to add a vertical loop with a version of the Texas skip with Melody hopping in and out, side to side at increasing speed. I admit that it became breathtaking to watch, and when added to the act it always ended to cheers and applause. Florence modified Melody's squaw costume so that she could move more freely.

Other new elements in those first weeks included Strong's bullwhip work, and reinstatement of the knife throwing with Lottie as target girl.

My instinct had not been wrong. Kit Strong made an enormous difference to us. He brought the authenticity and sense of danger that our presentation so needed. Under Florence's teaching, Melody's rifle skills increased to the point where she joined us as a second trick shooter.

We now had two versions of the act, one for the sideshow and one for the stage. For sideshow music we had our old Calliope but for theatres I had new band parts copied, as I felt this was where our future lay. I was confident that before too long, we'd have our chance with one of the circuits.

When business took me away, Jack would step into my boots with no great loss to our presentation. During a winter engagement at Northampton's Palace Vaudeville I'd planned to take a day in Leicester, where I'd commissioned a lithograph poster from Wilson's. We'd left the wagons in Eastbourne and travelled up to Northampton by train. In our digs that morning, Florence came to tell me that Lottie was indisposed.

I said, "What's the matter with her?"

"Nothing to concern yourself with, William," Florence said.

"Is she ill?"

"I said she's indisposed." Florence's sharp tone was warning me to press it no further.

"Well," I said, "you'll have to stand in for the flying knives."

"Kit wants Melody."

"Does he," I said.

I went to find Kit Strong. He'd found himself a quiet corner and made it his own, as was his habit. All he ever needed was his old Indian blanket, a pouch of tobacco, and a cheap edition of something to read. I don't think he drank. When it came to the act, he was always professional.

He looked up from his novel and I said to him, "Florence is the target girl tonight."

His face betrayed nothing.

Then he simply said, "You're the boss," and returned to his book.

Florence was not the target girl that night. Melody was, in defiance of my instructions, and the first I knew of it was when she walked onstage. Florence gave me some unlikely explanation about a last-minute emergency. I did not hide my anger. But it was late, and I would deal with the situation in the morning.

I hardly slept. I have never seen a family business that did not carry at least one idiot. I did not wish to be perceived as ours.

What happened in the morning only made it worse.

I came down to breakfast to find several copies of the *Echo* around the table. The paperboy had made his daily delivery, and Jack had been sent out for more. The *Echo*'s critic had attended the previous night's show and had singled out the James family act as the highlight of the turns, and Melody as our *'exquisite little Girl of the Golden West, a shot to rival*

Annie Oakley, an English Rose as brave in the face of bladed danger as any moving picture heroine'.

Who can complain in the face of success? But a leader whose decisions aren't respected is no leader at all, and here was fuel for further disrespect. I said my piece about trust and authority, and the company pretended acquiescence. The extra newspapers were shredded for cuttings and that evening saw a crowd at the Palace box office, all of whom had turned out to see our exquisite little Girl of the Golden West. With Lottie still indisposed, I had to concede and let Melody continue. Receipts for the week were up, and when the engagement ended the management gave us a modest bonus.

Nonetheless, at the end of the week I said, "Enough's enough. As soon as Lottie's well again, she goes back in the act."

To which Melody said, "I want to do it."

"It's Lottie's job," I said. "You don't take another performer's job."

"Since when?"

"Melody. Don't argue with me."

But you can imagine my disquiet. My word had been disregarded and no disaster had occurred. The opposite had happened. The real problem would arise the next time I made a leadership choice that someone in the company didn't care for.

I couldn't say for sure who'd undermined me; Florence had been the spokesman and Melody the most disappointed, but the disturbance had been started by Kit Strong, who'd then stayed silent throughout.

Melody knew better than to argue. But as surely as I'd been damaged as a leader, I'd been challenged as a parent. I could only hope that she wouldn't develop a will and a temper to match her mother's.

I did my best not to be unreasonable. As a sharp-shooter Melody was becoming the equal of Florence, and would soon surpass her in accuracy and speed. I gave her more gunplay to go with the rope tricks, and the act flourished. It took some persuasion to get Jack to fan the cards and hold them for the Poker Hand Split, but with each flawless shot his discomfort was diminished. Melody never missed. With Lottie back on the target, Strong added a blindfold and a second row of knives for an even bigger finale.

Lottie said to me, "It's a mistake to keep me up there, William. After the build-up with Melody I'm not the one they want to see."

Dear Lottie, she had none of a performer's jealousy. Or perhaps she just wanted someone else to face a blindfolded impalement artist every night. Whatever the case, I held out.

When there was some money in the kitty I took us all down to the studio at Beagles' where we posed in full costume for a set of cabinet cards. I ordered up a batch of the postcards with the intention that we'd sell them after each performance. I learned that Kit Strong was making himself some extra cash by appearing with his bullwhip at the stage door, where he'd tell a few tall tales and then split your card for a souvenir while you held it at arm's length.

As the warmer weather came, we went back on the road. Melody was already smitten with Strong, I think. Florence and Lottie were resistant to his doubtful brand of charm, but pragmatic about his importance to the troupe. Women in the audience were less reserved. I suppose they were moths at a safer distance from his flame. They saw a glamorous and world-weary figure who had seen sights and been to places that they would only read of in magazines or the novels of Elinor Glyn. No matter that he was a practised fabulist, and could be a consummate liar. During the roping tricks they no doubt imagined themselves in Melody's place.

I hardly dare think what they'd be imagining as the knives flew.

Things were going well. Most people still considered us more of a sideshow than a theatrical act, but that had begun to change. I should have been happy, but I was not. I might say that I was glad that Strong chose to spend so much of his time alone, as I was never easy in his company. And I'd often remember the strange warning that he'd given to me at our first meeting.

We had a gaff hand name of Jencsik. My father had taken him on and he travelled with us everywhere, as anything from driver to baggage master. One night at Hull Fair he came to me and said, "William, something's bothering me."

I said, "What would that be, Jimmy?"

"You know how Strong likes to open his tent to the audience after a show?"

I did. He sold his cards from the tent when we were on the road. Some he'd split with the bullwhip, some he'd just sign.

Jimmy said, "I looked in just now and the tent's full of children with Strong sitting there as naked as the day he was born."

"What?"

"Pointing out his scars," Jimmy said.

I rushed over. The tent flaps were down and any crowd was now gone. I found Strong alone and pulling on his jacket, getting ready to head into town. I repeated what Jimmy had told me and Kit Strong said, "He's mistaken."

"That's a hard mistake to make," I said.

"You'd better take that up with him," Strong said. "I have nothing to explain."

"No?" I said. "Consider this a warning, and I'm making a rule. No more of these private audiences after the show. Especially children. Or your impressionable young women."

"Especially?"

"We don't need rumours."

"Can I still sell my cards?"

"Sign them out front. It's better publicity."

"You're the boss."

"Am I? Sometimes I wonder."

"Don't wonder, William," he said. "Be clear. Your God-given job is to hold this show together. You brought me in. You're in control. If you ever let me walk away thinking I got the upper hand, then someday we'll both have reason to be sorry. And when the day comes, just remember how I warned you."

With that, he pushed his way past me and out of the tent.

*　　　*　　　*

AND WITH that, Sebastian lowered the pages and massaged his aching eyes. He'd lost track of the time. The daylight was all gone and the room's sole electric bulb made a poor substitute. For some time now the copy had been crying out for a fresh sheet of carbon paper, and the typist hadn't used one. There was more to read, but he'd reached the point where his mind was struggling to take it in.

Reluctantly, he laid the pages aside.

He'd resume in the morning. First light.

The Authentic William James
© Stephen Gallagher The Brooligan Press 302pp
ISBN 978 0 9957973 0 7

THE SEBASTIAN BECKER NOVELS

"That rare beast, a literary page-turner"—*Kirkus*

Chancery lunatics were people of wealth or property whose fortunes were at risk from their madness. Those deemed unfit to manage their affairs had them taken over by lawyers of the Crown, known as the Masters of Lunacy. It was Sebastian's employer, the Lord Chancellor's Visitor, who would decide their fate. Though the office was intended to be a benevolent one, many saw him as an enemy to be outwitted or deceived, even to the extent of concealing criminal insanity.

It was for such cases that the Visitor had engaged Sebastian. His job was to seek out the cunning dissembler, the dangerous madman whose resources might otherwise make him untouchable. Rank and the social order gave such people protection. A former British police detective and one-time Pinkerton man, Sebastian had been engaged to work 'off the books' in exposing their misdeeds. His modest salary was paid out of the department's budget. He remained a shadowy figure, an investigator with no public profile.

THE KINGDOM OF BONES

After prizefighter-turned-stage manager Tom Sayers is wrongly accused in the slayings of pauper children, he disappears into a twilight world of music halls and temporary boxing booths. While Sayers pursues the elusive actress Louise Porter, the tireless Detective Inspector Sebastian Becker pursues him. This brilliantly macabre mystery begins in the lively parks of Philadelphia in 1903, then winds its way from England's provincial playhouses and London's mighty Lyceum Theatre to the high society of a transforming American South—and the alleyways, back stages, and houses of ill repute in between.

"Vividly set in England and America during the booming industrial era of the late 19th and early 20th centuries, this stylish thriller conjures a perfect demon to symbolize the age and its appetites"

—New York Times

THE BEDLAM DETECTIVE

…finds Becker serving as Special Investigator to the Masters of Lunacy in the case of a man whose travellers' tales of dinosaurs and monsters are matched by a series of slaughters on his private estate. An inventor and industrialist made rich by his weapons patents, Sir Owain Lancaster is haunted by the tragic outcome of an ill-judged Amazon expedition in which his entire party was killed. When local women are found slain on his land, he claims that the same dark Lost-World forces have followed him home.

"A rare literary masterpiece for the lovers of historical crime fiction."
—MysteryTribune

THE AUTHENTIC WILLIAM JAMES

As the Special Investigator to the Lord Chancellor's Visitor in Lunacy, Sebastian Becker delivers justice to those dangerous madmen whose fortunes might otherwise place them above the law. But in William James he faces a different challenge; to prove a man sane, so that he may hang. Did the reluctant showman really burn down a crowded pavilion with the audience inside? And if not, why is this British sideshow cowboy so determined to shoulder the blame?

"It's a blinding novel... the acerbic wit, the brilliant dialogue—the sheer spot-on elegance of the writing: the plot turns, the pin sharp beats. Always authoritative and convincing, never showy. Magnificently realized characters in a living breathing world . . . Absolutely stunning"
—Stephen Volk
(Ghostwatch, Gothic, Afterlife)

"Gallagher gives Sebastian Becker another puzzle worthy of his quirky sleuth's acumen in this outstanding third pre-WW1 mystery"
—Publishers Weekly starred review

"Gallagher is an elegant stylist, a shrewd psychologist… a powerful storyteller with enormous range and depth"—Ed Gorman

NIGHTMARE, WITH ANGEL

After rescuing Marianne Cadogan from an incoming tide on a lonely and forgotten part of Britain's coast, ex-con Ryan O'Donnell is cornered into helping her escape a supposedly abusive father to reach the safe custody of her mother. Too late, he finds himself compromised, the subject of a trans-European manhunt while he struggles to deliver the child and prove his motives pure. The deeper in he gets, the more trapped he will become

"A world class, first-rate novel"   **—Elizabeth George**

"A moving, shocking, compelling psychological drama with a mesmerising plot… impossible to put down and, once read, impossible to forget"
                                                       —Booklist

THE BOAT HOUSE

A dark love story, and a disturbing tale of a divided soul. In the days leading to the fall of the Soviet empire, a young woman with a deadly secret slips unnoticed into the West. And when Alina Petrovna first appears in Three Oaks Bay it's clear that her frail, luminous beauty is likely to cause some ripples in the surface calm of the peaceful resort town. For Pete McCarthy, the boatyard worker who gives her shelter, she's an enigma. A complex, well-meaning young woman with a difficult past. Someone whose mystery deepens as the season gets under way, and the deaths by drowning begin...

"Gallagher handles the balance between mundane reality and stomach-turning horror with reassurance and offers a nicely twisted ending to boot. Highly recommended"
                                        —Nigel Kendall, Time Out

Also from The Brooligan Press

Tim Lees
FRANKENSTEIN'S PRESCRIPTION

Banished to an isolated rural hospital for killing a fellow student in a duel, Hans Schneider meets the mysterious Dr Lavenza and learns about Frankenstein's prescription—the secret of eternal life. Together, Schneider and Lavenza set out to collect the missing pieces of the formula. But they are not alone. From Germany to Rome, from Rome to Paris, to the failed and wretched Eden of an all-too-human God, a dreadful creature follows in their wake and brings destruction wherever they go.

"A philosophically insightful and literary tale of terror"
—Publishers Weekly

Laurence Staig
THE COMPANION

A broken church window, smashed in a bid to contain the power trapped within its stained glass... the desperate sobbing of a child who isn't there... When restoration expert Kit Farris moves into the adjoining Grange with his three daughters, how can he know what dark forces his work will unleash?

"An excellent book which celebrates and transcends genre. As much family story as ghost story. A tense drama of abuse, neglect and longing. An old-fashioned ghost tale with a modern edge, consciously a tribute to M R James in its setting and atmosphere. It echoes a book such as Margaret Mahy's The Changeover in its depiction of children rallying their defences against the urgency of adult appetites."
—The London Times

"It scared the life out of me"
—Philippa Pearce

l

Printed in Great Britain
by Amazon